Abducted by an Alien

Jonny Zucker

Illustrated by
Paul Savage

Titles in the Full Flight Variety series

Badger Publishing Limited
Oldmedow Road,
Hardwick Industrial Estate,
King's Lynn PE30 4JJ
Telephone: 01438 791037
www.badgerlearning.co.uk

2 4 6 8 10 9 7 5 3

Abducted by an Alien   ISBN 978 1 85880 932 8

Series Editor: Jonny Zucker
Publisher: David Jamieson
Editor: Paul Martin
Design: Jain Birchenough
Cover illustration: Paul Savage

Abducted by an Alien

Jonny Zucker

Illustrated by Paul Savage

Contents

Badger LEARNING

Chapter 1
Shelly's Story

When Shelly told our teacher Mr Tann she'd been abducted by aliens, he laughed.

He said, "Now now Shelly."

and, "I don't think so."

and, "It must have been a dream."

But Shelly wasn't having it.

"It was on my way home yesterday after school," she told him.

"I was going through the DIY store car park when there was a big flash of light. Suddenly I was in the air being sucked into this alien spaceship. I bumped my head when I got there."

"What did they look like?" asked Mr Tann, "were they green with three heads?"

"There was only one of them," Shelly told him. "He said his name was Zot."

"Well what did you talk to Zot about?" Mr Tann asked her, trying to hide his smile.

"I told him all about my cat Sam," said Shelly.

"Zot said he wanted to learn how to dance, so I showed him a few steps. Then I was dropped back down into the car park and I bumped my head again."

At the end of the lesson, Mr Tann went off smiling to himself, but I stayed talking to Shelly. The more she told me about the alien space ship, the more it sounded real.

But wait a minute! Aliens? Space ships? This was all stuff from TV and not real life.

"I want to believe you Shelly," I said, "but it just sounds like you made it up." Shelly pulled a face at me.

"OK Dan," she said, "Let's go home through the DIY store car park today and see what happens."

"I can't today," I lied. To tell the truth I was a bit scared.

"Alright then," grinned Shelly, "Tomorrow."

"OK," I said, trying not to show the fear in my eyes, "tomorrow it is."

Chapter 2
Up and Away

All of the next day in school I kept on thinking about the alien space ship.

Shelly must have made up the story, but what if...?

Mr Tann was asking me something but I was looking out of the window up into the sky.

"Well, Dan?" said Mr Tann, "what do you think?"

"I think Shelly made the alien space ship story up, but maybe she didn't and it's all true."

Mr Tann looked at me in a funny way.

"Dan, we are trying to learn about the Greeks, not talk more nonsense about alien space ships. Let me tell you something. There are no aliens. There are no alien space ships.

"Shelly told the story to have a bit of fun, didn't you Shelly?"

"NO!" shouted Shelly looking angry.

"Stop it," said Mr Tann, "Forget these silly stories and listen to the lesson."

"You'll see," whispered Shelly, glaring at Mr Tann.

After school, I started to walk home my usual way, but Shelly ran after me.

"Not that way Dan, this way," she said, turning me around.

We walked across the street and over to the DIY store car park.

"I'm going to watch from over there," Shelly told me, and she ran off to hide behind some dustbins.

"Thanks for nothing," I called to her.

I stood in the car park for a few minutes, looking up into the sky, but nothing happened.

There you are, I told myself, *she made up the whole thing.*

I looked over to the dustbins where Shelly was hiding, and called, "Let's go home."

As soon as I said these words, there was this great flash of white light in the sky and I suddenly felt myself being sucked into the air.

Chapter 3
The Space Ship

As I was pulled into the sky, I made up
a letter to my mum in my head.

Dear Mum,

I've been abducted by an alien space ship.

I may be back a bit late for supper,
because I don't know how long I'll be
needed up there.

Hope you are OK about this.

Yours,

Dan.

I found myself sitting at a big metal table inside a giant space ship. There were blue and red buttons all over the place and thousands of tiny white lights on the roof.

"Ow," I said, rubbing my head.

"Sorry about that," said a voice, "People always bang their heads when I bring them up here."

I looked up and came face to face with an alien. He was sitting on the other side of the table.

He was about my size with big, flat ears, very round eyes and long, thin fingers.

"Hi," he said, "Welcome to my space ship. My name is Zot."

"I know your name," I told him, "My friend Shelly met you the other day."

"Oh her," said Zot. "She told me no one would think she was telling the truth about coming here."

"Our teacher laughed at her when she told the story," I said.

"What's a teacher?" asked Zot.

I pulled a face. "They come from another planet. No offence to you, but they are weird people."

"I'd like to meet one," said Zot.

"I don't know if you would," I laughed.

Suddenly Zot looked very sad.

"Is everything OK?" I asked.

"Not really," said Zot, "I've been sent down to Earth to find out all about you lot, and so far I haven't found out many things.

"Shelly just talked about something called a cat and showed me some dance steps. If I don't bring back lots more facts, they may send me away again."

"OK," I said, "I think I know where to begin."

"Where?" he asked.

I took off my trainers and waved them in the air.

"This is where!" I shouted.

Chapter 4
Trainers

"What are those funny things from your feet?" Zot asked.

"They're called trainers," I told him.

"What do you do with them?" he wanted to know.

"You run in them," I replied, "Would you like to try them on?"

He nodded his head, so I handed them over to him.

He put the trainers on his feet, which were about my size.

He walked about in them. He jumped up in them.

Then he started to run around the space ship. He was like a flash!

Then he asked about my baseball cap. I let him put it on and he held it for a bit. Then he put it on his head.

He wore it...

Forwards...

Backwards...

Sideways...

Then he put it on his hand, his foot and his ear.

Next Zot pointed at my headphones.

I told him to put them on.

I tapped 'play' on my phone and the music started.

Suddenly Zot began to dance in a most funny way.

"Shelly showed me these steps," he shouted.

"They look really cool," I lied.

"Oh no," I shouted, looking at my watch. "My mum will kill me if I'm not home soon."

"Thanks for showing me all those things." Zot smiled. "I think they'll be pleased with me on my planet. And I can teach them all to dance."

I wanted to say maybe that wasn't such a good idea, but there was suddenly a flash of white light.

I landed back in the car park with a bump. I rubbed my head.

"Sorry," I heard a distant voice call.

Chapter 5
Big Trouble

"What is it now?" asked Mr Tann, looking angry.

We were in the playground doing PE. I was running next to Shelly and you can guess what we were talking about.

"Er... we were talking about that alien space ship, Mr Tann," I said. "You see the thing is, now I've been there too."

Mr Tann looked even more angry.

"That's it!" he shouted. "Stop running you two, and go to the Head Teacher's office!

"I want you to tell her how you are driving me mad with your made-up stories about a silly alien space ship."

We walked across the playground and back into school.

"She'll go mad with us," I said to Shelly.

We tapped on the Head Teacher's door.

There was no answer.

"The Head Teacher's not in for the rest of the day," said Mrs Burns, popping her head round her door.

"Was it something I can help with?"

"No, not really," I said.

"Come back and see her tomorrow," Mrs Burns told us. We walked back to the playground.

"What will we tell Mr Tann?" I asked Shelly.

"We'll tell him the Head Teacher wasn't there," she said

"But he'll still be angry with us and he'll never believe our story about Zot and the space ship," I replied.

Suddenly Shelly began to smile.
"I've got a plan," she said.

Chapter 6
Serves Him Right

Mr Tann was cross with us for the rest of the day.

In the afternoon, we went to see him.

"If it's about the alien space ship, forget it," he said without looking up from the books he was marking.

"You'll still be going to the Head Teacher tomorrow."

"No, it's not," Shelly told him. "It's about those cars we were making the other day. We want to make a new and bigger one."

Mr Tann looked up. He loved making things.

"OK," he said. "If you really want to, but I don't have any more wood."

"You could get some from the DIY store after school," smiled Shelly.

Mr Tann looked at us. "Not a bad idea" he said, "And you do really want to make this car?"

We both nodded.

After school, we ran to the DIY store. We hid behind the dustbins and waited.

About half an hour later, we saw Mr Tann arrive in his car. He stepped out and started to walk across the car park.

Before he'd got far, there was a great white flash of light and we saw Mr Tann being lifted off the ground.

"At least Mr Tann will believe us now," Shelly said.

A few seconds later we heard a bump.

"Sorry," we heard a distant voice call.

Then we heard some loud music starting up, and Zot shouting, "Let's dance!"

We looked at each other and began to laugh.